# Brighteye and the Blue Moon

**Daisy Meadows**

ORCHARD

## For Isla and Evelyn Blyth

★ ★

## Special thanks to Adrian Bott

ORCHARD BOOKS

First published in Great Britain in 2020 by The Watts Publishing Group

1 3 5 7 9 10 8 6 4 2

Text copyright © 2020 Working Partners Limited
Illustrations © Orchard Books 2020
Series created by Working Partners Limited

A CIP catalogue record for this book is available from the British Library.

ISBN 978 1 40835 706 4

Printed and bound in Great Britain by Clays Ltd, Elcograf S.p.A.

The paper and board used in this book are made from wood from responsible sources.

Orchard Books
An imprint of Hachette Children's Group
Part of The Watts Publishing Group Limited
Carmelite House
50 Victoria Embankment
London EC4Y 0DZ

An Hachette UK Company

www.hachette.co.uk
www.hachettechildrens.co.uk

# Contents

Aisha and Emily are best friends from Spellford Village. Aisha loves sports, whilst Emily's favourite thing is science. But what both girls enjoy more than anything is visiting Enchanted Valley and helping their unicorn friends, who live there.

## Silvermane

Silvermane and the other Night Sparkle Unicorns make sure night-time is magical. Silvermane's locket helps her take care of the stars.

Dreamspell's magic brings sweet dreams to all the creatures of Enchanted Valley. Without her magical powers, everyone will have nightmares!

**Dreamspell**

**Slumbertail**

With the help of her magical friends and the power of her locket, Slumbertail makes sure everyone in Enchanted Valley has a peaceful night's sleep.

Kindly Brighteye is in charge of the moon. The magic of her locket helps its beautiful light to shine each night.

**Brighteye**

Spellford

Enchanted Valley

Enchanted Cottage

Golden Palace

An Enchanted Valley lies a twinkle away,
Where beautiful unicorns live, laugh and play
You can visit the mermaids, or go for a ride,
So much fun to be had, but dangers can hide!

Your friends need your help ~ this is how you know:
A keyring lights up with a magical glow.
Whirled off like a dream, you won't want to leave.
Friendship forever, when you truly believe.

## Chapter One
# Midnight Howl

It was bedtime, but Aisha and her best
friend, Emily Turner, weren't ready to
go to sleep just yet. They were sitting
on the floor of Aisha's cosy bedroom in
Enchanted Cottage, playing another
game of cards. Emily had spent the entire
week with Aisha, sleeping over every

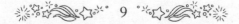

night and having a great time.

"Come on, girls," Aisha's mum called from downstairs. "Time for lights out."

The girls sighed as they abandoned their game for the night, but climbed into their beds.

After ten minutes Aisha still felt wide awake. So did Emily. Although the light was off, a golden glow shone even brighter than the silver moon. The girls both gasped with delight. "Our keyrings!" they said together.

Their little crystal keyrings, in the shape of unicorns, were presents from Queen Aurora. She was the wise and friendly unicorn who ruled over Enchanted Valley, a secret magical world where Aisha and

Emily had had many adventures together.

When the keyrings glowed like this, it meant Queen Aurora was calling them.

Aisha quietly scrambled out of bed. "Time to go back to Enchanted Valley!"

"I can't wait!" Emily said with glee.

They snatched up their keyrings and pressed them together. A swirling fountain of rainbow sparkles whirled around them, lifting them up off the floor.

Quick as a shooting star, the sparkles began to fade away and their feet settled back down on to lush green grass.

Emily looked around and saw they had landed on the slope of a hill they knew well. Queen Aurora's palace stood before them, a beautiful golden building with eight tall turrets that spiralled like unicorn horns.

Aisha looked up into the dark sky with a sigh. "It's still night in Enchanted Valley! It's been night here for ages now."

"We've got to put a stop to it," Emily sighed. "Once and for all!"

Every evening in Enchanted Valley, the four Night Sparkle Unicorns would combine the power of their magical lockets to bring the night. Then they did the same thing at dawn, to bring back the

day. But ever since the wicked unicorn Selena had stolen their lockets, Enchanted Valley had been trapped in an unending night.

Aisha took big strides up the hill and saw the full moon above the palace towers, shining like a silver coin. With a loud rattle of chains, the drawbridge dropped. There, standing on the other side, was Queen Aurora! Even at night-time, they could see the way her coat rippled with all the colours of a dawn sky, and they could make out the glitter of the little crown she wore on her head. The girls ran up to her and threw their arms around her neck.

"Welcome back!" Queen Aurora

laughed. "I've
missed you both."

"We've missed
you too," answered
Emily.

"But is there
anything wrong?

Has Selena been causing trouble?" Aisha
asked.

"I didn't call you because of a problem
this time," Aurora explained with a smile.
"It's more of a fun reason. You see ... even
though this is the longest night we've ever
had, there is one good thing about it."

"What's that?" Emily asked eagerly.

"The full moon is here already!" said
Queen Aurora. "So we can have our

monthly campfire party. I thought maybe you both might like to come."

Emily and Aisha glanced at each other and grinned. "Yes, please!" both girls chorused.

"Wonderful! Follow me," Queen Aurora said. She trotted in front of them, leading the way down the hill. Aisha and Emily bubbled over with excitement.

They soon found themselves deep in thick woods full of the lovely scents of pine needles and moist night air. Although there were dark shadows everywhere and strange noises all around, the girls knew they had nothing to fear while they were with Queen Aurora.

"Look!" Emily cried. Up ahead, firelight

flickered between the tree trunks and they could hear many happy voices chatting and singing together. Aurora led them into an open glade bathed in moonlight. In the centre was a large pit containing a roaring campfire, and glimmering firefly lanterns hung from the low branches of the surrounding trees.

The party was already in full swing. Unicorns, phoenixes and even a family of tiny gnomes all sat on logs around the

campfire, singing songs and sipping hot
chocolate. Hob, the little green goblin
who had often made the girls potions to
help them on their quests, was playing
a lively jig on his fiddle. Marshmallows
floated above the campfires, suspended
there by some unseen magic.

Aisha clapped her hands. "It's lovely!"

"Off you go! Have fun." Aurora
beamed.

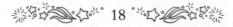

"Look over there," Emily told Aisha. "Isn't that Dreamspell?"

"Yes!" Aisha exclaimed. "And the rest of the Night Sparkle Unicorns, too. Come on!"

As they run towards their friends, Emily could see that Dreamspell, Silvermane and Slumbertail were all wearing the lockets the girls had helped to rescue from Selena. Only Brighteye, the moon

unicorn, was still missing hers. They needed all four magical lockets to make daytime come again.

Aisha was just about to say hello when something made her freeze in her tracks – a long, mournful, eerie howl. She felt goose pimples rise all over her body. Emily shot Aisha a frightened look and reached for her hand.

"Was that … a wolf?" Aisha whispered.

Emily glanced into the dark shadows between the trees, expecting glowing eyes to appear there.

"It definitely sounded like one," she said, her voice quaking with fear. "And who do you think wolves would work for?"

Aisha shuddered. "Selena!"

## Chapter Two
# Lights Out, Moonwolf

Aisha and Emily huddled anxiously together by the fire until Brighteye stepped forward. "Don't worry," she said soothingly. "That howl is just our friend Milo the Moonwolf. He's on his way."

"Moonwolf?" said Aisha.

"Yes! He lives on the moon," said

Brighteye. "Milo is very important. During the day, Aurora guards the valley from Selena. But at night, Milo the Moonwolf comes here from his den to keep watch over us all."

Brighteye pointed to the sky with her horn. Emily could just make out a faint moonbeam shining down over the trees, like a shaft of silver mist.

As she watched, something appeared in the distance, giving off a strange glow – a four-legged shape, with a huge head and a great hairy tail! It was galloping down the moonbeam. As the shape came closer, it grew larger and larger.

Emily and Aisha squeezed each other's hands. "I didn't know wolves could be so big!" said Emily, still a little scared.

They watched as Milo the Moonwolf
leapt off the moonbeam and landed
in the middle of the glade with a
tremendous thump. He turned his
shaggy head from side to side, looking
at all the creatures who were gathered
there, waving.
"Hello, Milo!"
they called.
"Welcome
back!"

Some of the
creatures ran
up to give him
a snuggle or
pat his head.

He gave them all a wide grin. His long tongue lolled out of his mouth happily, and the girls giggled. Suddenly he looked more like a big friendly dog than a scary wolf!

"He seems nice," Aisha whispered.

"And so pretty," said Emily. Milo's fur wasn't just glowing, it was as bright as the full moon. His whole body seemed to be made from moonlight.

Milo took another step towards the Night Sparkle Unicorns, which wasn't easy, because so many of the party guests were still crowded around him. Some of the little animals had even climbed up on to his back.

Brighteye bowed her horn in greeting.

"Milo," she said, "this is Aisha and Emily, the wonderful girls we told you about!"

Milo leaned his enormous head in for a closer look. Aisha gave a little gasp at the sight of his luminous eyes.

"How lovely to meet you both at last!" Milo said in a deep, rumbling voice. "Thank you for coming to my party."

"*Your* party?" asked Aisha.

"Is it your birthday?" asked Emily.

The moonwolf chuckled and shook his head.

"No," Queen Aurora explained. "We have a campfire party in Milo's honour every full moon — because he is such a brave and loyal moonwolf."

"So it's a thank-you party!" Aisha said.

No wonder everyone was making such a fuss over Milo.

The moonwolf sighed happily, and his misty breath was like a lovely cool night breeze that tickled the girls' cheeks. "It's so good to see all my friends! It can be lonely, patrolling the fields and the forests at night while everyone else is fast asleep."

"But it's obviously such an important

job," Emily said.

"I bet even Selena would think twice before starting any trouble, with you around," Aisha agreed.

But just at that moment, a crash of thunder ripped through the trees. The girls felt the ground shake under their feet. A bright blue-and-white scribble of lightning zigzagged down through the sky and suddenly Selena appeared!

She gave a wicked whinny as she shook her twilight-blue mane over her shining

silver coat. Her eyes flashed dangerously, and all the party guests squealed and ran for cover. Selena's little owl servant, Screech, came flapping along by her side, holding a wooden box in his talons.

"Having fun, are we?" Selena crowed. "Well, fun's over now! I still have the Moon Locket, and you're never getting it back. Screech, open the box!"

Screech didn't seem to have heard

her. He looked around and blinked his big yellow eyes. "Are you all having a party?" he asked.

"I said *open the box*, you overstuffed cushion!" shrieked Selena.

Stuck in the box's keyhole was a little silver key on a long chain. Grumpily, Screech turned the key with his beak and flipped the lid open with his claw.

Light poured out from the box. Inside, lying on the velvet lining, was a small round object that looked just like the full moon.

Brighteye gasped. "My locket! Give it back!"

"Not a chance," gloated Selena. "This box is off to a secret hiding place. You'll

never, ever find it. And even if you did,
you'd never get it open. Because I'll have
the key!"

Screech grabbed the key, flew up and
hung the chain around Selena's neck.

"If you don't make me queen, the
locket will stay shut away. Then the
moon will disappear for ever," Selena
said. "You know

what that means?
No moon, no
moon*wolf*! Your
overgrown lapdog
will vanish quick
as ... as ... this
marshmallow!"
And with that, she

snatched a marshmallow from a nearby fox cub and gobbled it up.

Milo snarled, baring his teeth. He began to lope towards Selena.

"Get away, you mangy mutt!" she exclaimed.

Aisha saw a glimmer of fear in Selena's eyes.

"Hurry up, Screech. We are leaving!" said Selena.

The pair of them flew off, vanishing into the depths of the forest and taking the box containing the locket with them.

Suddenly, everything seemed much darker. The stars were still shining overhead, but only a few hints of light showed through the tree branches. The fire

was down to its embers. It wasn't nearly enough to light the clearing.

Everyone in the glade huddled closer around the campfire and cast fearful glances into the shadows.

"Look!" Emily pointed up into the sky. "The moon's gone!"

Where the moon had hung a moment ago, silver and bright, now there was nothing but darkness. Screams and gasps rang out.

Luckily, the girls were standing right next to Milo, whose coat shone like a lantern. They squeezed closer to him.

"Don't worry, everyone!" Milo's powerful voice boomed out. "I'm here to protect you. There's nothing to be afraid of."

"Thank goodness for you, Milo," Emily said.

But then Aisha gasped and pointed. "Emily, look!"

Milo's light, which had been so clear and strong, was flickering.

"Milo!" they cried together.

Then Milo's light went out completely. Just like the moon.

## Chapter Three
# The Dark Forest Monster

As quickly as it had vanished, Milo's light came back on. But it was definitely dimmer than before.

Brighteye paced back and forth. "I was afraid this would happen," she said. "Milo is made out of moonlight. If we can't bring the moon back …"

"… then I'll just keep fading and fading until there's nothing left of me," Milo finished. His tail drooped and his ears sagged.

Emily and Aisha looked at each other with concern.

"Milo disappearing is awful enough by itself," whispered Emily, "but Queen Aurora can't protect Enchanted Valley at night like he does. What'll happen to the kingdom if he's not here?"

"I don't want to find out," Aisha whispered. "We've got to save him."

Emily gave Milo a cuddle while Aisha went and stroked Brighteye's mane reassuringly. "Don't worry," she said. "We'll help you get your locket back.

Then Milo will be just fine."

Silvermane stepped forward. "It looked to me like they were heading for the Dark Forest," she said.

There were little squeaks of fright from the creatures in the clearing. Even the unicorns looked scared.

"What's so bad about the Dark Forest?" asked Emily.

Silvermane took a deep breath. "A monster lives there!"

"A monster?" Aisha asked, shivering. "So there really are monsters, even here in Enchanted Valley?"

Slumbertail nodded and whispered, "I've heard it has a hundred eyes!" She glanced around as if she feared the monster was watching her right then. "It wouldn't dare leave its lair while Milo is here," she said. "But now that his light's starting to fade, who knows what it might do?"

"We're still going," Emily said bravely.

"Of course we are," agreed Aisha. "If there are monsters around, it's even more important that we get the locket back, and fast!"

"Wait!" Brighteye said. "I'll go with you. It's my locket, after all."

"I'll come too," rumbled Milo. "To light your way." He turned aside, closed his eyes and murmured, "… while I still can."

Brighteye knelt down so the girls could climb on to her back. Then the party guests, along with Queen Aurora, all

wished them good luck.
Leaving the flickering
lights of the campfires
behind, they headed
through the trees and
into the darkness of the
waiting forest.

Soon, the sounds of the gathering died
away. Nothing broke the silence but
the clip-clop of Brighteye's hooves, and
Milo's paws crunching on the bracken.

Milo trotted beside Brighteye, looking
keenly into the dark. Suddenly he
stopped. "I can smell musty feathers," he
said. "I think … yes, it's Screech! He came
this way. I have his scent!"

"Hooray!" cheered Emily. "Well done,

Milo!"

With the moonwolf leading the way, they rode on into the forest. They had to squeeze between huge trees that loomed overhead like great swooping ghosts. Chattering, buzzing, squeaking noises filled the night air as they travelled deeper and deeper into the woods. Sometimes they heard a distant hoot, or a soft rustling nearby, but they could see no one

else through the darkness.

Aisha huddled up to Brighteye and shivered. "What if Silvermane and Slumbertail were right?" she whispered to Emily. "What if there really is a monster?"

Emily hugged Aisha tighter around the waist. "Milo's here," she reminded her. "He won't let anything happen to us."

But just then, Milo's whole body blinked out again, from his nose to his

tail. It reminded Emily of the light in her parents' kitchen, which sometimes flickered before it turned on properly.

When it returned, Milo's light was even dimmer than before. They could only make out the closest trees now. He gave a little whimper so Emily ruffled his fur.

"What's that, up ahead?" Brighteye said.

Bobbing along in the air, weaving through the trees, was a little white shape.

"It's not the monster, is it?" Aisha said warily.

"I think it's Screech!" exclaimed Emily.

Milo sniffed the air. "It's him all right."

"Can't catch me, you silly old wolf!" mocked Screech, and flapped away.

Milo growled.
"You three wait
here. I'll grab that pesky
owl and bring him back
in two beats of a moth's
wing!"

Before any of them could say another
word, Milo had gone bounding off after
Screech. His huge, dimly glowing body
vanished into the distance.

Aisha, Emily and Brighteye were left all
alone in the darkness, right in the middle
of the forest.

For a few moments, nobody said
anything. They just huddled together,
their hearts beating fast, while the spooky
night-time sounds rustled and hissed all

around them.

"I hope he's OK out there," Aisha said. "Milo? Milo! Can you hear me?"

No answer came back.

"I wish I could fly us out of here," Brighteye said, "but we can't leave Milo behind. And besides, it's too dark to see where I'm going."

Nearby, a swaying branch creaked with a sound like an old door slowly opening.

Emily squeezed Aisha's hand nervously. Then she gasped as she saw a glow of light.

"Oh, thank goodness!" Aisha burst out. "Milo's coming back."

To both the girls' relief, they could soon see that it really was the moonwolf trotting back towards them. But something wasn't quite right. He was walking in a weird, stiff way, as if he had a leg cramp.

"Are you OK?" Aisha asked him.

Milo blinked. "Me? Oh! Yes, I'm fine. I just, er, tripped. That's it. I was chasing after that owl, and I tripped over a tree root. He can fly very fast, you know."

Aisha and Emily exchanged a look. Once Milo's back was turned, Emily whispered, "I'm not sure he *is* fine."

"He's acting strangely," Aisha agreed.

"Where's Screech?" Brighteye asked.

"I'm afraid he got away. He's very clever," Milo said. "But I did hear him say something about a cave nearby. That must be where Selena hid the locket."

"A cave?" Aisha said anxiously, wondering what might be lurking inside.

"Yes, and I think I know where it is. Come on!"

They followed Milo through the Dark Forest to a spot where the ground rose up to form a rocky wall. Sure enough, there was an arched cave mouth with tree roots dangling down above it. Inside, it was pitch black.

"In you go," Milo said.

"Can't you go ahead and light the way?" Aisha suggested.

"I'll be right behind you, shining my light from there," Milo promised.

The cave's ceiling was low so Aisha and Emily climbed off Brighteye's back. Hand in hand, they took their first steps in. Water dripped nearby, *plip-plop*. A root touched the back of Emily's neck and made her yelp.

Step by nervous step, they made their way deeper and deeper into the cave. Milo's light, shining behind them, seemed dimmer than ever.

Then, from the pitch blackness up ahead, they heard a sound. Something was stirring. Something huge, that rustled and flapped and scratched.

Suddenly, eyes were peering at them out of the darkness. Big, round, yellow eyes. Dozens and dozens of them.

"A hundred eyes!" cried Emily.

Aisha fought hard not to scream. "The monster! It's real!"

# Chapter Four
# Scaredy-Wolf

Milo yelped in alarm. He turned around and ran out of the cave.

"Milo, come back!" Aisha yelled. "We need you to protect us!"

"I thought he was supposed to be b-brave," Brighteye stammered.

The girls stroked Brighteye's neck.

"Well, we'll just have to be brave ourselves," Emily whispered.

"The locket might be here," said Aisha. "And if we've got to face the monster, at least we'll do it together."

"OK," Brighteye whispered, her voice wavering.

As they listened to the sound of Milo crashing clumsily through the undergrowth, they stood side by side, ready for anything.

Suddenly two of the eyes broke free from the rest as something fluttered forwards. Aisha squinted, trying to see what it was. She made out beating wings, little hooked feet, a curved beak, feathery tufts like ears …

"It's an owl!" she cried. "That's all. Just an owl. No bigger than Screech."

More pairs of eyes came towards them, and the girls saw they didn't belong to a monster at all. They belonged to more owls – dozens and dozens of them!

"Hello!" the girls said together.

The owl in front gave a sweeping bow. "Hello to you too-hoo-hoo! My name is Blink," he said. "I'm so happy to meet you! Finally, a

visitor to our humble cave."

Aisha and Emily looked at one another and giggled. Even Brighteye joined in. How had they been so scared of these nice owls?

"We thought you were a monster!" Aisha told Blink.

"A monster?" Blink tipped his feathery head. "Is that why nobody ever wants to

come and visit us?"

A few of the owls behind him hooted sadly, their feathers drooping.

"Yes!" said Brighteye. "We all thought a monster

lived here."

"But now we know it's you, you'll make loads of new friends!" said Emily.

"In fact," said Aisha, "there's a party in the clearing in the woods right now. Go and introduce yourselves!"

The owls all began to bob up and down and ruffle their feathers excitedly. "Thank you so much," Blink hooted. "We can't wait to meet some new friends!"

"We'd take you to the party but we have to find Selena and Screech, and Brighteye's locket," said Emily. "Goodbye! See you all soon!"

"Goodbye!" came the chorus of hooting voices.

Aisha, Emily and Brighteye made their

way out of the cave, feeling a lot less scared than they had been when they entered.

"We should have known there was nothing to be scared of," Emily said. "Just like we had nothing to be afraid of when we met Milo."

"Poor Milo. *He* must have been really frightened, to run away like that," Aisha said.

"Yes," said Brighteye, cocking her head in thought. "It's so unlike him. I've never seen him get frightened like that."

"Well, it *was* pretty scary in the cave," Emily said.

"But Milo's been in dark caves before, lots of times," Brighteye said firmly.

"If I didn't know better, I'd say it wasn't Milo at all."

Aisha and Emily looked at each other. They both had the same thought at the exact same moment. Screech had a secret power to change into the shapes of other creatures.

"Oh no," they said together. "Not again!"

Just then, they spotted Milo bounding back towards them. When he saw the girls he came to a sudden stop and stared, open-mouthed.

"What are you doing here?" he asked. "Didn't the monster get you? I mean … thank goodness the monster didn't get you."

"Drop the act, Screech," Emily said. "We know it's you."

In a puff of magic, Milo disappeared and Screech was suddenly there in his place.

"Took you long enough to work it out!" he taunted.

Brighteye stamped her hoof. "Where's the real Milo? What have you done with him?"

Instead of answering, Screech just flew away, hooting with laughter.

From somewhere in the forest, a sad howl rang out.

"Milo!" Aisha yelled.

"Climb on my back, quickly!" said Brighteye.

Aisha and Emily held on tight and
Brighteye took them through the forest.
It was hard to see, so she couldn't go very
fast. All they could do was follow the
howls. Soon, Emily spotted a silvery glow
shining up from the ground.

Brighteye headed for the light and
stopped. They were right at the edge of a
deep pit!

And there on the floor of the pit,
looking miserable, was Milo the

Moonwolf.

"Milo! Thank goodness we've found you!" Aisha called out.

"What happened?" Emily shouted.

"Screech and Selena set a trap!" Milo growled. "I fell for it. Or rather *into* it."

Aisha looked down. "Can you climb out?" she called.

"I tried," Milo answered. "The walls are too steep."

Emily had an idea. "Brighteye, can you fly him out?"

"I don't think so," Brighteye said sadly. "He's too big for me to lift."

"Maybe there's something in the forest that can help us," Aisha said. "Let's have a look."

Although it was nearly pitch dark, with only the light from the stars to see by, Aisha and Emily headed into the forest.

"Oof!" Aisha said as she tripped over something half-hidden in the ferny undergrowth. "What was that?"

Emily looked down. "It's a log!"

"Perfect!" said Aisha. "Milo can use this to climb out of the pit! Brighteye, can you help us push this log over there?"

Together the three of them shoved the log over to the pit.

Brighteye gave it a good hard kick with her hind hooves. It tilted over and slid down.

Milo pressed on the log with his paw, testing its strength. "Perfect!" he said. "Just like a moonbeam to run along."

He scrambled up the log and burst out triumphantly in a shower of dry leaves. Aisha and Emily gave a cheer, then hugged him.

"Thank goodness you're safe," Aisha said.

But as they stepped back, they saw Milo's light had faded. A lot! And not only had his glow dimmed, but the edges of his fur were almost invisible now. They could see the trees through his body!

Aisha and Emily shared a worried glance. They were running out of time to save Milo.

# Chapter Five
# The Watery Hiding Place

Milo sniffed the air. "I've got Screech's scent again," he said.

Brighteye laughed. "He can change his shape, but he can't change how he smells!"

"He won't get away this time," Milo growled.

Brighteye and the girls followed Milo through the Dark Forest once more. Soon they heard the gurgle and splash of running water nearby. Moments later, they emerged through a gap in the trees and found they were on the bank of a stream. Even without the moon overhead, the water glittered in the light from the

stars, as if it were full of a million silver fishes.

"This is where the scent trail ends," Milo said. He leapt across the stream, sniffed, shook his head and leapt back over again. "It doesn't carry on from the other side, either. I can't tell where Screech went from here."

"Maybe he flew up into the sky and hid the locket in a tall tree?" guessed Brighteye.

"Or maybe he followed the stream through the forest?" suggested Emily.

But Aisha noticed something the others hadn't. She pointed the other way, where the stream flowed down a rock face in a little waterfall, creating clouds of mist.

"Remember when Selena said she had a secret hiding place for the locket?" Aisha said. "What if it's behind that waterfall? That would be a great hiding place!"

"It's got to be worth a look!" Emily said. "Let's go!"

The waterfall was like a fine,

shimmering curtain. Aisha cautiously reached through with one arm. Sure enough, there was a hollow behind the waterfall!

She took a deep breath, bent her knees and jumped through the cold water.

Emily and Brighteye followed her through, shivering as the water splashed them.

Milo jumped through the waterfall last and squeezed in to join them, but they could tell right away that something was wrong. Instead of a shining, pearly moonwolf, he was a dark, shadowy, wolf-shaped smudge. They could hardly see him at all any more.

"We've got to find that box fast, and get Milo his light back!" Aisha whispered to Emily.

"Yes, but how?" Emily replied. "It's so dark in here. I can't even see my hand in front of my face!"

Just then, another voice spoke from the back of the cave — a familiar, grumpy, hooting voice. "Gah!" it squawked. "You found my hiding place!"

"Screech?" gasped Aisha.

"Well, that's it," Screech groaned. "Selena's going to be so cross with me. She'll get a new helper, and I'll have to go back to spending every single night all by myself without any friends."

"Is that why you were helping her?" Emily asked gently. "Because you didn't want to be alone?"

Screech sighed. "Yes. I know Selena isn't very nice, but everyone else goes to sleep at night. I just get so bored with nobody to talk to or play games with."

"I understand," came Milo's faint voice. "I get lonely during the long nights, too."

Aisha suddenly felt an idea lighting up her mind like a brilliant spark. "Hey, Screech? If we promised to take you to meet a lot of new friends, would you help us instead of Selena?"

The whole cave echoed with flapping noises as Screech beat his wings in excitement. "Of course I would! It's a deal!"

"Thank you, Screech!" Emily cheered. "The first thing we need to do is to find that box. Can you tell us where it is?"

"Hmmm," said Screech. "Hoo. I definitely hid it in here somewhere. But it's so dark, I don't know how I can find it again."

"We need some light!" Aisha said.

"I'm sorry," whispered Milo. "My light is all gone."

"Let me try," Brighteye said. She was quiet for a second, then her horn lit up with a very faint light. The girls could see Brighteye's face for just a moment, before being plunged into darkness again.

"It's no good," Brighteye gasped. "Without my locket, I can't make it last."

"Wait!" Aisha said. "Screech, can you change into Milo, the way he looked before Selena made the moon disappear?"

"Of course!" Screech said proudly.
"I can change into anything!"

Instantly, the whole cave lit up as
Screech shifted into Milo's form. The light
that shone from his body was as bright as
the full moon had been.

"Well done, Screech!" yelled Aisha.

Then Emily gasped. She'd spotted the
box under the very
rock ledge that Screech
had been sitting on
moments before! She
quickly scooped it up,
cradling the box in
her hands.

"Got it!" she said.

"Now we just have to open it."

Aisha glanced at Milo, who was nothing but a shadow now, and said, "We need to do it fast, or Milo might vanish completely!"

# Chapter Six
# Party Crashers

"There's only one problem," said Emily. "Selena has the key, and we don't know where she is!"

"And we don't have time to go searching for her!" cried Aisha.

Emily held up the box and peered closely at it. "Maybe we can get it open

without the key," she said. "I know! Hob has all sorts of magical potions and things. He might know something we can do."

"Good thinking!" Aisha said. "We saw him at the party, playing his fiddle, remember? Let's go back there and ask him to help."

Brighteye bent down. "You girls get on my back. Screech, if you stay in Milo's form and light the way, we can see where we're going and gallop back through the forest."

"Happy to!" Screech said.

"Thanks, Screech," Emily said, patting him on the head. He blinked in surprise, then smiled.

They burst through
the waterfall and
thundered off through
the trees. Brighteye's
hooves pounded the
mossy ground and

Screech, still looking like Milo, took the
lead, banishing the long shadows that
loomed ahead. Emily clutched the box,
so it wouldn't get shaken out of her grasp.
And though none of them could see the
real Milo now, they could tell by the
leaves flying up along the path that he
was running beside them.

It was a wild, breathless ride. The
girls held on to Brighteye's neck as she
galloped. The forest was so huge and so

dark that the girls sometimes felt sure they would get lost, but Brighteye never stopped or paused for even a second. She directed Screech confidently as they raced along.

"Don't worry," she gasped. "Trust me. I know the way."

Sure enough, they soon saw the distant glimmer of firelight. They were back at the party!

But as they drew closer to the wide clearing, strange sounds reached their ears. There was no more music and no laughter. Instead, they could hear squeals and cries of fear, and the hasty footsteps of several creatures running away at once.

"Our friends are in trouble!" Aisha cried.

"Let's go and help," said Emily.

But Brighteye stopped in her tracks. "Wait. We should be careful. Let's see what's happening before we go charging in."

Moving as quietly as they could, they hid behind a tree so they could watch without being seen.

Emily gasped as she finally saw Selena in the middle of the forest clearing, stamping her hooves and

bucking her head! All the party guests were cowering in terror.

"What a lovely party!" Selena mocked. "Shame there's no moonwolf to enjoy it!" She pranced around in a circle, a huge smirk on her face. "Who's going to protect you now he's all faded away? Nobody, that's who! The kingdom is as good as mine! You silly creatures may as well bow down to me now. I'm your new queen!"

In the darkness nearby, Milo gave a whisper of a growl … fainter than a fading dream.

"He's almost out of time," Aisha warned.

Brighteye said, "Look, Selena's still got the key round her neck! This is our chance to get it. But how?"

Aisha thought hard. "I've got an idea," she said. "Remember when Selena first saw Milo, and he growled at her? She was scared silly of him."

"That's right!" said Emily.

"So why don't we get Screech to keep on pretending to be Milo and chase her right past where we're hiding? We can fly up as she goes by, and grab the locket!"

"OK," said Screech, readying himself.

"I hope this works, just to see the look on her face!"

As Brighteye hid behind the tree, Screech went bounding into the clearing. He charged right up to Selena, bared his teeth and let out a growl so loud it made her mane flutter.

Selena stared. Her eyes went as wide as pufflebunny tails.

"Whaaaaat? This can't be!" she howled. "You're meant to be all fizzled out! Argh! Get away from me, you mangy mutt!"

She reared up, flailing her hooves wildly. All the party guests cheered as Screech barked and growled at her.

Suddenly, Selena leapt from the ground and took flight, soaring over the party guests' heads.

But Brighteye, Aisha and Emily were prepared. As Selena came flying in their direction, Brighteye rushed up through the air at her. "Now, Aisha!" she called.

Aisha held on to Brighteye's mane with one hand and reached out for the key with the other. As Selena passed by, she grabbed at the key. Her fingers brushed the metal but closed on empty air. She had missed!

Selena flew up higher, cackling at the top of her voice. "Nice try, silly girl!" she shouted. "You'll never get the key from ..."

A high-pitched whistle sounded from down below, startling everyone – even Selena.

Emily could hear an uncanny rustling as the trees began to shake.

"Something's coming from the Dark Forest!" she shouted.

"I don't know what it is," Aisha added, "but it sounds big!"

The creatures at the party cried out together, "Monster!"

## Chapter Seven
# In a Flap

The treetops quivered. The branches shook.

Suddenly, with a great whirring of wings, dozens and dozens of owls rose up from the forest. They swept and soared through the sky above Selena, their wide wings spread out like the sails of a whole fleet of ships.

"It's Blink and the owls from the cave!" shouted Aisha.

"They must have come to the party, just like we said," added Emily.

There were so many owls filling the sky over the clearing that Selena couldn't push through them. They were trapping her in like the lid on a sandwich box. She had to fly lower, her hooves almost brushing the highest trees.

"Out of my way, you feathery rats!" Selena yelled. "Don't you know royalty when you see it?"

"Get ready for another go at that key, Aisha!" said Brighteye.

"Ready," Aisha said firmly.

Brighteye rushed through the sky, heading straight for Selena.

This time, Selena didn't see them coming. She was too busy trying to force her way through the barrier of beating owl wings. "I said *move*!" she howled.

"Now!" yelled Brighteye.

As Brighteye flew past Selena, Aisha

reached for the key, closed her fingers tightly around it and tugged the chain right off Selena's neck.

"I've got it!" she whooped.

Emily shoved the box under her arm and reached out. "Quick, pass it to me!"

Aisha's heart was pounding. Careful not to drop the key, she pressed it into Emily's hand. Emily slid it into the lock and twisted. With a click, the box flew open.

The Moon Locket sat inside on a little velvet pillow. Bright moonlight poured out from it, misty and magical.

Emily took it from the box and  quickly hung it around Brighteye's neck.

A beautiful sight filled the sky as the moon suddenly blazed with light once more, flooding the clearing and shining on the upturned faces of the girls and creatures. The circling owls hooted happily. Their gliding bodies and beating wings made dancing moon-shadows on the ground below.

Selena let out a furious shriek. "Gah! You meddling girls! Think you've won just because you found the Moon Locket, do you? Well, I'm just getting started!" She snorted crossly. "Screech and I will be back, you mark my words!" She looked around. "Where is that blasted bird, anyway?"

But there was no reply.

"Screech?" Selena bellowed. "I can't find you among all these owls! Where have you gone?"

Screech changed back into his owl form and fluttered up towards Selena.

"I'm right here," he said. "But I'm not going anywhere. Not with you."

"Oh yes you are," Selena said, "if I have to drag you out myself!"

She flew down towards Screech, who trembled at the sight of her.

Suddenly, a powerful voice roared out from among the party guests. "He said he didn't want to go with you, Selena. Leave him alone!"

Milo strode out from the crowds, his body glowing with bright moonlight.

Selena let out a little high-pitched noise, as if she were a mouse instead

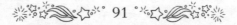

of a unicorn.

"In fact, you'd better leave all of us alone," Milo growled. "Or ELSE!"

Emily and Aisha cheered. "Milo's back!" they shouted.

Selena cringed. Turning toward the girls she sneered, "You think that overgrown dog can protect you from me?"

"Actually … yes," grinned Aisha.

"Ha! Well, dog or no dog, you haven't seen the last of me!"

With a crash of thunder, Selena flew away over the trees and into the sky. They all watched as she grew smaller and smaller, until she was no more than a tiny dot.

# Chapter Eight
# Campfire Funtimes

"Whoopee!" cried Hob, tucking his fiddle under his arm and throwing his hat into the air. "Hooray! She's gone!"

Laughter, cheering and applause broke out all around.

Brighteye flew down into the clearing, carrying Aisha and Emily on her back.

The girls climbed off into the middle of the delighted crowd. Everyone wanted to hug them and say thank you.

Then the crowds parted to let Milo through. The girls ran up to him and gave him a great big cuddle, burying their faces in his thick, glowing fur.

"I'm so glad you're OK!" Aisha said.

"We were scared you'd be gone for

ever," said Emily.

"I'm fine now, thanks to you," Milo said. His huge tail wagged happily.

Queen Aurora stepped forward, with a delighted smile on her face. Behind her came Dreamspell, Slumbertail and Silvermane, each with their lockets glittering proudly on their chests. Brighteye went to join them.

"Well done, girls," Aurora said. "You've saved Enchanted Valley once again!"

"We couldn't have done it without our friends, Brighteye and Milo," said Emily.

"Or our new friend, Screech!" Aisha added.

Queen Aurora looked up to the trees. All the owls from the Dark Forest had perched in the branches. They sat in shy, feathery rows, watching the festivities.

"It looks to me like you made quite a

few new friends!" Queen Aurora said.

"Yes, we did!" Emily said proudly. "Can I have everyone's attention, please?"

The party guests turned towards Emily and Aisha, quietly waiting to hear what Emily had to say.

"We'd like to introduce you all to the owls of the Dark Forest!" Emily said, with a grand flourish. "Everyone thought the hundred eyes belonged to a monster, but

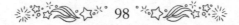

it was really these lovely owls."

"And they'd really like to get to know you!" Aisha added.

The owls bowed and all the party guests clapped or cheered, as relieved laughter spread through the crowd.

"I can't believe it," said Silvermane. "The monster wasn't even real!"

Blink flew down and landed on Aisha's shoulder. "If any of you would like to

come and visit us in our cave, we would love to see you-hoo-hoo. Everyone's welcome."

"I already know someone who'd like to visit," said Aisha. "Screech!"

Screech flapped forwards and perched on her shoulder. "Hello," he said eagerly. "I had no idea there were other owls in Enchanted Valley! I'm a screech owl. What kind of owls are you?"

"We're all night owls," explained Blink. "We've never met a screech owl before! You can come and stay in our cave any time you like."

"Can I? Oh, thank you!" Screech fluttered up and down joyfully. "I can't wait. This is going to be such fun!"

Nobody could remember a better full moon campfire party than this one. The owls of the Dark Forest mingled with all the other creatures and were soon chatting away, making friends and telling stories. Aisha and Emily toasted marshmallows over the golden flames and joined in with the traditional unicorn campfire songs. But of all the people and creatures at the party, no one had more fun than Screech.

"He's a changed owl," Aisha whispered to Emily.

"It's funny, really," Emily whispered back. "All this time, he's been pretending to be other creatures. But now that he's being himself, he's having the time of his life!"

As the embers of the campfires began to die down, the four Night Sparkle Unicorns gathered in the middle of the glade and touched their horns together. A deep chime rang out.

At long last, the first rays of dawn began to shine in the east. A beautiful melody echoed through the forest. Queen Aurora was singing.

"What's that gorgeous song?" Emily

asked Brighteye.

"It's the song of welcome to the sun," Brighteye said. "Queen Aurora sings it every morning."

Fresh cheering broke out across the camp. The night was finally coming to an end, and it would soon be daytime in Enchanted Valley once again!

"I suppose that means you have to go home now," Aisha said to Milo.

Milo yawned very wide. "That's right. I've loved meeting the two of you, but it's been a very long night, and I ought to get back to the moon. I'm ready for a good day's sleep!"

Brighteye smiled. "Let's get you home, then." Her locket glimmered with light. The next moment, a strong moonbeam streamed down from the sky.

Everyone waved goodbye to Milo as he trotted up the moonbeam.

Aurora turned to the girls. "You must both be tired, too, after all your adventures!"

Emily and Aisha nodded sleepily.

"It's definitely past our bedtime." Aisha gave a great yawn. "I've never stayed up

until dawn before!"

"But we'd love to come back again soon," Emily said. "Just call us if Selena gives you any more trouble, OK?"

"I will," Aurora promised. "But for now, I have a special gift for you both, to say thank you for all your help!"

She gave them each a crystal charm in the shape of a glittering star. Emily and Aisha gasped.

"Thank you!" Emily said.

"They're beautiful!" Aisha added.

The girls added the stars to their

keyrings, where they hung next to the other charms Aurora had given them. Every time they looked at the shining stars, they would remember the Night Sparkle Unicorns and all the adventures they had had together.

The girls said a drowsy goodbye to everyone at the party.

"Sleep well," said Aurora. "See you very soon!"

Aurora bowed her horn. Shimmering sparkles whirled up and around the two girls. Before they even had time to blink, they were back in Aisha's bedroom.

It was still night-time in the ordinary world as not a moment had passed since they left. The full moon shone brightly through the curtains, and their new star charms twinkled in its friendly light.

Emily sighed happily as she climbed into bed. "That was so much fun!"

"It really was," Aisha said. "And do you know what the best part is?"

"Hmm?" said Emily, who was already almost asleep.

"I'm finally sleepy!"

Emily laughed and closed her eyes. Even though she was tired out, she couldn't wait for their next adventure in Enchanted Valley to begin.

The End

Join Emily and Aisha
for more fun in …
## Sparklebeam's
## Holiday Adventure
**Read on for a sneak peek!**

"Get ready, Emily – here comes a big
wave!" cried Aisha Khan. She was lying
face-down on her surfboard, gripping the
edge. As the wave came towards her, Aisha
leaped to her feet. She crouched, ready to
ride the wave as it lifted up her surfboard.

Emily Turner, Aisha's best friend,
grinned up at her. She was lying on her
surfboard too, but the girls weren't really
in the sea – they were in the living room
of Enchanted Cottage, where Aisha lived
with her parents. Both girls were giddy
with excitement, because their families

were going on holiday together! Outside, their parents were packing the Khans' car. Soon they would set off for the coast, to stay in a seaside cabin. But it was pouring with rain, and their parents were wearing anoraks over their summer clothes.

### Read
# Sparklebeam's Holiday Adventure
### to find out what's in store
### for Aisha and Emily!

# Also available

**Book Five:**

Daisy Meadows

Silvermane Saves the Stars

**Book Six:**

Daisy Meadows

Dreamspell's Special Wish

**Book Seven:**

Daisy Meadows

Slumbertail & the Sleep Pixies

**Book Eight:**

Daisy Meadows

Brighteye & the Blue Moon

# Unicorn Magic

## Look out for the next book!

Daisy Meadows

# Unicorn Magic™

Three stories in one

Sparklebeam's Holiday Adventure

From the author of
RAINBOW MAGIC

If you like
Unicorn Magic,
you'll love ...

## Welcome to Animal Ark!

Animal-mad Amelia is sad
about moving house, until she
discovers Animal Ark, where vets look
after all kinds of animals in need.

Join Amelia and her friend Sam for a
brand-new series of animal adventures!